THIS BOOK BELONGS TO

THANKS TO PHILIPPA, MY FAMILY,
MARTHA, JULES AND EVERYBODY AT NOBROW.

PAPERBACK EDITION FIRST PUBLISHED IN 2015 BY FLYING EYE BOOKS,
AN IMPRINT OF NOBROW LTD. 27 WESTGATE STREET, LONDON, E8 3RL.

ORIGINALLY APPEARING IN PRINT IN 2010 AS HILDAFOLK. © 2010 NOBROW LTD. AND LUKE PEARSON.

4 6 8 10 9 7 5

PUBLISHED IN THE US BY NOBROW (US) INC

PRINTED IN POLAND ON FSC® CERTIFIED PAPER
ISBN: 978-1-909263-78-9

ORDER FROM WWW.FLYINGEYEBOOKS.COM

HILDA'S DRAWINGS APPEARING ON PP. 32-35 BY MARTHA NORMAN.

LUKE PEARSON

HILDA
AND
THE TROLL

FLYING EYE BOOKS
LONDON - NEW YORK

SPLENDID...

MUM!

HEY!

WHAT'S WITH YOU? WHY DO YOU KEEP COMING IN HERE UNINVITED?

LEAVE HIM BE HILDA. I THINK HE COMES TO KEEP WARM OR SOMETHING. AND BESIDES, HE BRINGS US WOOD.

WELL I STILL THINK HE'S VERY RUDE. AND A WEIRDO TOO..

..DON'T YOU HAVE YOUR OWN HOUSE?

A SEA SPIRIT!

POOR THING. IT MUST HAVE DRIFTED DOWN THE FJORD AND GOTTEN LOST.

I WONDER WHERE IT'LL END UP.. I WONDER IF IT MATTERS..

HEY.. THIS ROCK.. IT KIND OF LOOKS LIKE.. LIKE...

A TROLL ROCK!

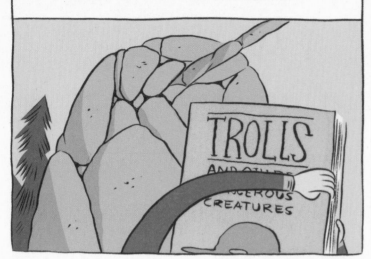

BY DAY, IT'S NOTHING BUT A PECULIAR LOOKING ROCK. BUT BY DARKNESS...

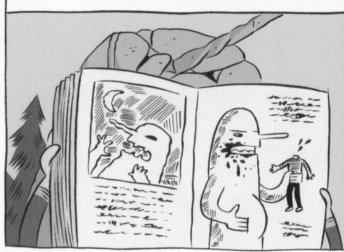

...IT TAKES THE FORM OF A FIERCE AND POWERFUL TROLL!

I MUST DRAW IT- I'VE NEVER HEARD OF THEM COMING THIS FAR DOWN THE MOUNTAIN BEFORE.

LUCKILY I WAS PREPARED FOR THIS PRECISE EVENTUALITY.

I NEED YOU TO TAKE THIS BELL, TWIG-

-AND TIE IT AROUND HIS NOSE. THAT WAY, IF HE BUDGES, WE'LL HEAR IT.

NOT THAT HE WILL...

..YOU KNOW, JUST IN CASE A CLOUD GOES OVER OR SOMETHING..

GOOD JOB! NOW, TO DRAW!

I KNEW IT! WE'RE SAVED!

I'M SURE THEY WON'T MIND IF WE LET OURSELVES IN. WE ARE IN DISTRESS.

HELLO? IS ANY-BODY HOME?

WHUMF

I'M READY.

OR I WOULD BE...
WHAT'S HE WAITING
FOR? HE JUST KEEPS
SWINGING AROUND
THAT INFERNAL
BELL!

Jingle

Jingle

I THINK YOU HAVE IT.
ACCORDING TO THIS, TROLLS
CAN'T STAND THE SOUND
OF A BELL'S TOLL. THE
BELL TRICK IS NOWADAYS
COMMONLY ACCEPTED TO
BE RATHER CRUEL.

TROLLS

...DIDN'T
YOU READ
THAT FAR?

TROLLS

WELL THAT EXPLAINS WHY HE FOLLOWED ME
HERE... THE POOR THING CAN'T REACH.
HE NEEDS HELP GETTING IT OFF!

HEY! MY
SKETCHBOOK!
(I forgot all about it..)

YOU BROUGHT
IT ALL THIS
WAY TO GIVE
IT BACK?!

I KNEW TROLLS WERE NICE
I JUST KNEW IT! I THOUGHT
IT ALL ALONG! COME
INSIDE, I'LL DRAW YOU ANOTHER
PICTURE AS A THANK
YOU GIFT! WE CAN BE
FRIENDS, BEST FRIENDS!
I'VE ALWAYS WANTED TO
BE FRIENDS
WITH A -

..OH.

GOOD
BYE
THEN..

OH NO, THE
PICTURE'S ALL
RUINED NOW
ANYWAY.

IT WAS
ALL FOR
NOTHING
...

and although they will often mimic the regular stones that litter their territory, they are far from undetectable. They are frequently distinguishable by the hints of a face or the characteristically long nose, although the more devious trolls will actively attempt to conceal this feature.

Left, photograph of a petrified troll with concealed nose (photographer/date unknown). Above, an artist's interpretation of the unpetrified specimen.

The petrification process is not a pleasant or comfortable one for the rock troll, with the level of discomfort varying wildly. Larger trolls tend to take it in their stride, while for smaller and weaker specimens the effect can be permanent. It's generally accepted however that all those vulnerable to the sun's effects strive to avoid it when possible. Even those species not susceptible to petrification appear to take a dislike to it. It is for this reason that trolls tend to make their homes in the shadows of mountains, deep in forests and most commonly, in caves. Even at night it is rare to encounter a troll too far from the safety of its lair for fear of being caught out by the approaching dawn.

TROLLS & BELLS

It has long been known that trolls have a seemingly irrational fear of the sound of ringing bells. Unlike sunlight, the sound appears to have no physiological effects on the creatures, except for those resulting directly from the psychological distress the ringing causes them.

Historically, this has been exploited to great effect by humans who have found themselves in conflict with trolls, both as a method of personal self-defence and on a larger scale. Settlers arriving in the unspoiled wildernesses around the Nornfjords would first erect temporary wooden bell towers, to secure the area in preparation for building. Cities such as Trolberg maintain a large number of permanent bell towers with a regular ringing schedule to keep the native trolls a safe distance from their walls.

In the past, travellers would hang small bells in the mouths of caves that were believed to be home to trolls, both as a warning to fellow travellers looking for shelter and to potentially prevent the trolls from leaving their lair.

Similarly, when setting up a camp, travellers would search the immediate area for suspicious looking rocks and hang a bell from any nose-like protrusions they came across. If any of the stones began to stir when night fell, the camp would be alerted. However, in recent

THIS STRANGE AND BEAUTIFUL WORLD. I'D BE CONTENT TO SIT HERE FOREVER AND SIMPLY EXPERIENCE IT.

I'M A COMPLICATED PERSON, WITH MANY SIDES TO ME.

END.

SKETCHES

These are a selection of drawings from my sketchbooks, all done during the development of this comic. —LUKE

water spirit

troll stone

the wood man.

trolls

birdcat.

Some early sketches featuring the Wood Man wearing clothes and a cat with a beak who would eventually become Twig.

"Tall Hilda"

Ideas for scenes to include in the story.

This one didn't quite make it.

Pt Pt Pt Pt Pt Pt Pt Pt Pt

oh my...

There seems to be a mysterious giant lurking in the background of this one...

Two rough comic pages.

This is the precise moment that Twig stopped being a cat and became a fox.

Make him a teensy fox instead.

HILDA FINDS HER WORLD TURNED UPSIDE DOWN AS SHE FACES THE PROSPECT OF HAVING TO LEAVE HER SNOW-CAPPED BIRTHPLACE FOR THE HUM OF THE CITY.

IN HILDA'S NEXT ADVENTURE

MUM! DO WE HAVE ANY BOOKS ABOUT GIANTS? OLD GIANTS?

BUT WHY DO THE HIDDEN ELVES WANT HER TO LEAVE? WHY IS IT THAT ONLY SHE CAN SEE THEM? AND WHO IS THE GIANT THAT TURNS UP IN THE NIGHT?